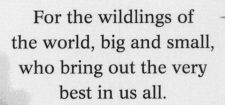

For the wildlings of
the world, big and small,
who bring out the very
best in us all.
R. B.

To all the
Freddies and Fredas
out there who
wouldn't fit in.
I. E.

ORCHARD BOOKS

First published in Great Britain in 2020 by The Watts Publishing Group

1 3 5 7 9 10 8 6 4 2

Text © Rachel Bright, 2020 • Illustrations © Izzy Evans, 2020

The moral rights of the author and illustrator have been asserted

A CIP catalogue record for this book is available from the British Library

ISBN HB 978 1 40835 009 6 • ISBN PB 978 1 40835 007 2

Printed and bound in China

FSC
www.fsc.org

MIX
Paper from
responsible sources
FSC® C104740

Orchard Books, an imprint of Hachette Children's Group
Part of The Watts Publishing Group Limited
Carmelite House, 50 Victoria Embankment, London EC4Y 0DZ
An Hachette UK Company
www.hachette.co.uk • www.hachettechildrens.co.uk

Free-Range
FREDDY

Rachel Bright   Izzy Evans

ORCHARD

Once upon a chicken coop,
a mother hen called Peggy
Waddled up the chicken steps,
to lay a little eggy.

She sat and warmed it every day   inside a straw-made beddy.

It took some days and then some nights
until that egg was ready.

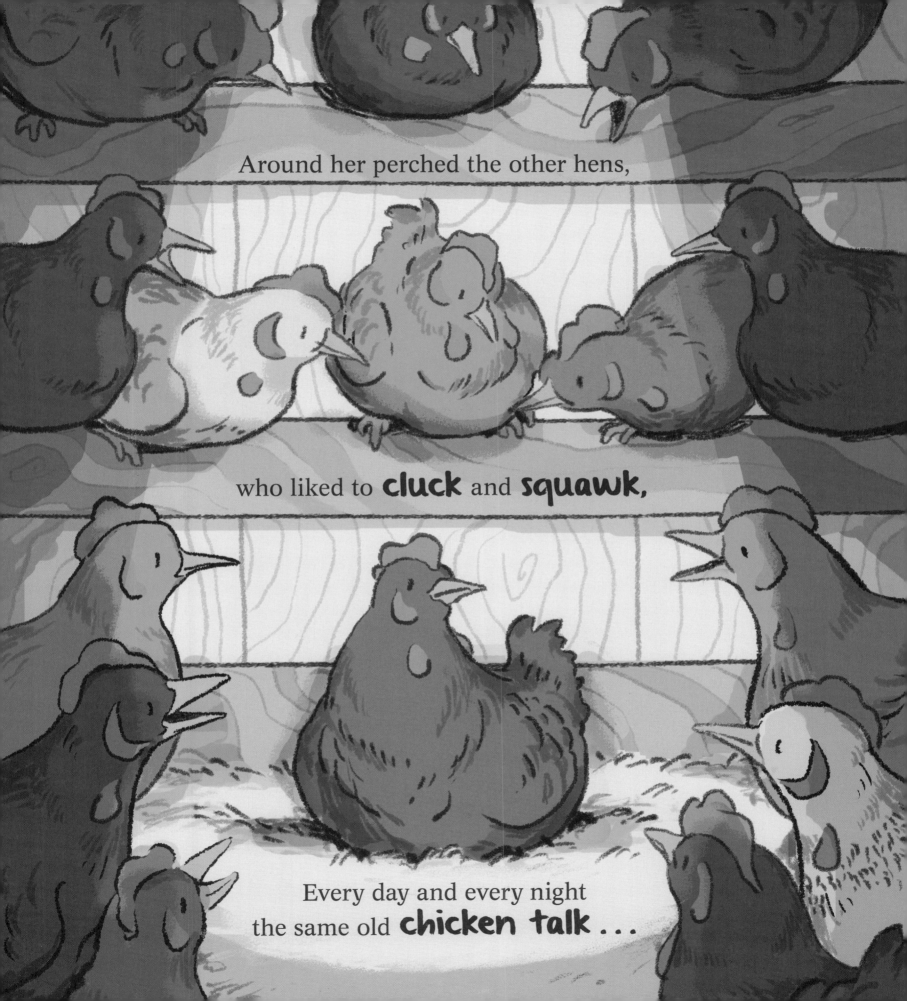

Around her perched the other hens,

who liked to **cluck** and **squawk,**

Every day and every night
the same old **chicken talk . . .**

"We know this egg's a good one!
Just think what it might bring . . .

Perhaps a finely feathered queen
or handsome cockerel king!"

Then one very happy day,
that egg began to **hatch.**
The chickens huddled round to see
whose guess that chick would match.

Out it came:
a **crick,** a **crack,**
a beak peeked from the eggy.

And all at once **exploded** forth . . .

a multi-coloured
Freddy!

His eyes were rather **bulbous**.

His feathers **full of fluff.**

His wattle **wibble-wobbled.**

And his legs?

Not **long** enough!

And stretching out
his wonky wings,
he opened up his beak,
Announcing his arrival
with a feisty,
high-pitched

shrieeeek!

Well! That very ordered hen-pen
was thrown into a spin.
They'd never seen a wilder chick . . .
This chick would
not fit in!

He floppled round the hen-pen,
he flew in crazy shapes.
He woke the chickens up at night
by getting into scrapes.

His cartwheels on the coopy roof,
made them feel quite **jumpy.**

He made a **noise** and made a **mess . . .**

which made them **super grumpy.**

BUT a strange thing
started happening, a tiny bit at first . . .

The hens began to whisper,

"We suppose it could be worse."

And the more he doodle-did his thing, the more his sunshine spread . . .

Their tutting turned to **chuckles**
and they threw him
smiles instead.

Then when he sang his silly songs,
they sometimes joined in too.
Un-cooping their *own* music
made them **happy**
through and through.

You see, instead of being proper –
a behaved, well-mannered sorty . . .

He let out all their **wild sides,** and made them rather **naughty!**

A king indeed he had become,
he'd managed something rare.

He brought the very best thing out,
in every chicken there.

Yes, Freddy was one wild chick,
that's what those hens would say.
But we're ALL a *little* wild sometimes.
And guess what?